For Janetta, Jude and all my friends at Frances Lincoln,
with love from Laurence Anholt

For all children
who have more than
one nest. x

J.C.

JANETTA OTTER-BARRY BOOKS

First published in Great Britain in 2013 and in the USA in 2014 by
Frances Lincoln Children's Books, 74-77 White Lion Street, London N1 9PF
www.franceslincoln.com

A catalogue record for this book is available from the British Library.

ISBN 978-1-84780-323-8

Illustrated with watercolours

Set in Cochin and FF Tusj

Printed in Dongguan, Guangdong, China by Toppan Leefung in July, 2013

3 5 7 9 8 6 4 2

Two Nests

Laurence Anholt

Illustrated by
Jim Coplestone

F

FRANCES LINCOLN
CHILDREN'S BOOKS

Two little birds,
funny as can be,
sitting at the top
of a cherry tree.

One called Betty,
one called Paul,
the autumn leaves
began to fall.

The wind was cold,
Betty was chilly.
"Build me a nest, dear –
don't be silly."

The winter was long
but the nest was snug,
two little birds
like bugs in a rug.

THEN...

Up came the sun,
bright as can be,
and the blossom came out
on the cherry tree.

Betty said, "OOPS!
I feel a little funny,
there's something rumbly
in my tummy."

Out popped an egg,
the egg went PLOP!
Then Betty Bird
sat on top.

They waited a month,
they waited a week,
then the egg went CRACK!
And the egg went CREAK!

Out came a baby,
funny as can be,
running all around
in the cherry tree.

Betty sang a song
for Baby Bird,
the sweetest song
you ever heard…

"The sun is bright,
the sky is blue,
three little words, dear –
I
LOVE
YOU."

Then all the animals
came to see
those three funny birds
in the cherry tree.

BUT...

the birds were **large,**
the nest was small,
there wasn't room
to fit them all.

Paul and Betty
were grumpy as can be.
They squabbled at the top
of the cherry tree.

Two little birds said,
"It might be best
if we build Daddy
ANOTHER NEST."

Paul packed his bag
and everybody cried.
They made another nest
and he hopped inside.

Paul felt bad,
Betty felt sad,
and Baby Bird said,
"I want my dad."

THEN...

Betty sang a song
for Baby Bird,
the sweetest song
you ever heard...

"You had a home,
    now you have two,
four little words, dear –

WE
BOTH
LOVE
YOU."

Up came the sun,
warm as can be,
the cherries tasted sweet
at the top of the tree.

Baby said, "OOPS!
I'm all in a tizzy,
I feel a little fluttery,
I feel a little dizzy.

Mummy, Mummy!
What are these things?
They look just like
a pair of **wings**!"

At last that baby
found what's best,
flying back and forth
from nest to nest.

Then everybody
ran to see,
as Baby flew over
the cherry tree.